THE LOUKOUMI

MAKE A DIFFERENCE

FOUNDATION

The Loukoumi Make A Difference Foundation is a 501c3 non-profit organization formed with the consent of the New York State Department of Education to teach children to make a difference in their lives and the lives of others. The Foundation has established programs on bullying awareness, encouraging children to do good deeds and to pursue their dream careers. Each October the Make A Difference With Loukoumi project unites over 100,000 children nationwide to do good deeds. The project has received the USA Weekend National Make A Difference Day Award, Tegna's National Make A Difference Day All-Star Award and The Point of Light Award. Based on the project the Loukoumi Foundation has sponsored The Make A Difference With Loukoumi Exhibit at The Westchester Children's Museum, a national literacy project benefiting St. Jude Children's Research Hospital and a Good Deed of the Month Curriculum in 300 schools. The Loukoumi Foundation also sponsors its national Dream Day contest making kids' career dreams come true for a day. The Loukoumi programs were featured in the Make A Difference With Loukoumi TV Special that aired on FOX stations nationwide. For more on The Loukoumi Foundation please visit: www.LoukoumiFoundation.org

It was a beautiful spring day!
Loukoumi and her friends were
playing baseball in the park.

Fistiki was at bat. Dean was catching. Marika, with her speedy legs, covered the outfield, and Loukoumi was pitching. It was the last inning! Fistiki was down to his final strike! Loukoumi tossed the pitch. Fistiki swung and knocked the ball over the fence - Home run!

"Way to go me!" Fistiki cheered, doing his victory dance.
"Great game!" Loukoumi said, congratulating her friend.
"I'm hungry," Dean added.

"I brought lunch," Marika said, taking sandwiches, carrot sticks, apples, juice boxes and cookies out of her picnic basket.

The friends talked and laughed and ate,
while Fistiki bragged about his home run.

When Fistiki was done, he dropped his juice box on the ground and started walking away.

"Let's play another game!" He said.

"Not so fast!" Marika scolded.
"A park is a place for one and all
to have a picnic or play some ball.
But it's up to us to keep it clean,
plant a tree and make the world green.
The trash will mount, if we don't act,
and the environment will suffer, that's
a fact!

It's up to us to make this right,
before it's too late and we lose the fight.
So let's support nature, what do you say?
Let's make a difference and let's start today!"

13

The friends then looked around and noticed garbage everywhere. Bottles, cans, bags and wrappers were littered across the park.

"Wow, I never realized how bad the park looked before," Loukoumi said.

As the friends started cleaning up, Police Officer Gus appeared.

"What's going on?" Fistiki asked.

"The town is closing the park because no one takes care of it. Look here, even the birds have left," Officer Gus said, pointing to an abandoned nest.

"I'm sorry, but you're going to have to find somewhere else to play."

"How could this happen?" Loukoumi asked.

17

"It takes a lot of work to preserve the environment," Marika said. "I visited a rainforest in Hawaii once and it was one of the most beautiful places I have ever seen because people worked hard to preserve its natural beauty. We can do that here too."

"I'll go to Hawaii," Fistiki said. "I have always wanted to surf the waves!"

"Stop joking, Fistiki! This is serious!" Marika said.

"We can work in our own homes to conserve energy," Loukoumi noted, "by not leaving the water running too long."

"Or by closing lights and electrical appliances when we do not need them," Dean added.

"And we can recycle!" Fistiki chimed in.

20

"Great ideas!" Marika said.
"Let's make a difference and let's
start today with our park."

Loukoumi and her friends did not want to lose their park and they did everything they could to make it better.

Marika planted new trees and flowers.
Loukoumi cleaned up the trash.

Dean collected all the bottles and cans
and Fistiki painted the park benches.

As the team put the finishing touches on the baseball field, Officer Gus returned.

"You kids did an amazing job," he said, "and the town has agreed to keep the park open."

Loukoumi and her friends cheered while Fistiki did his victory dance again.

The following week, the town threw a re-opening party for the park.

"We would like to thank Loukoumi, Fistiki, Dean and Marika," Officer Gus said, "by presenting them our green medals of honor and naming the town league "The Make A Difference Baseball League." The crowd cheered!

Difference

League

Loukoumi and her friends were
so happy and Loukoumi said:

"A park is a place for one and all
to have a picnic or play some ball.
But it's up to us to keep it clean,
so we planted a tree, and made the park green.
The trash will mount, but we will act
and help the environment, that's a fact!
So let's continue to support nature, what do you say?
Let's make a difference every day!"

About the Author

Loukoumi Saves a Park is Nick Katsoris' eighth book in the Loukoumi series. The book series has received two iParenting Media Awards, two Mom's Choice Awards, the Family Choice Award and two World Cookbook Awards. Proceeds from the books have benefited children's charities including St. Jude Children's Research Hospital.

Based on the themes in his books, Katsoris sponsors several programs including the *Loukoumi* Dream Day contest, which grants kids the opportunity to spend the day in their dream careers. He also sponsors Make A Difference With Loukoumi Day, based on his book *Loukoumi's Good Deeds* (narrated on CD by Jennifer Aniston), which rallies 100,000 kids each October to do a good deed on national Make A Difference Day. The project received a national USA Weekend Make A Difference Award, Tegna's Make A Difference Day All-Star Award and The Point of Light Award.

In 2014, Katsoris founded The Loukoumi Make A Difference Foundation to teach children to make a difference in their lives and the lives of others. The Foundation's first project was the Make A Difference With Loukoumi TV Special which aired on FOX, NBC and ABC stations across the United States and Mega-TV internationally. The Loukoumi Foundation also sponsors Good Deed programming at its exhibit at The Westchester Children's Museum and at over 300 schools.

Katsoris is a New York attorney and President of the Hellenic Times Scholarship Fund, which has awarded over two million dollars in scholarships. Nick is also a board member of Chefs for Humanity, has worked on a Loukoumi literacy awareness program with the National Ladies Philoptochos Society, and is a member of Kiwanis International. Nick resides in Eastchester, New York, with his wife, Voula, a real estate attorney, and their children, Dean and Julia.

About The Loukoumi Book Series

- **LOUKOUMI** – *"From candy to a character! The story of a lamb who gets lost trying to find her way to America."* – THE NEW YORK TIMES
- **GROWING UP WITH LOUKOUMI** – *"Charming! Beautiful! Gives Confidence!"* – Martha Stewart, The Martha Stewart Show
- **LOUKOUMI'S GOOD DEEDS** – *"Teaches kids that you can make others happy by doing something nice!"* – Entertainment Tonight
- **LOUKOUMI'S GIFT** – *"Jennifer Aniston narrates the tale of Loukoumi the lamb as she goes about her day learning to help others in need!"* – PEOPLE Magazine
- **LOUKOUMI'S CELEBRITY COOKBOOK** – *"Recipes that make celebrities feel like a kid again."* ABC-TV's The View; *"A fun nostalgic cookbook!"* – Oprah.com
- **LOUKOUMI & THE SCHOOLYARD BULLY** – *"An engaging, cheerfully illustrated story with a classic moral."* – KIRKUS Reviews
- **LOUKOUMI IN THE BASKET** – *"Children's stories with morals!"* – Ladies Home Journal; *"Loukoumi is darling!"* – New York Daily News

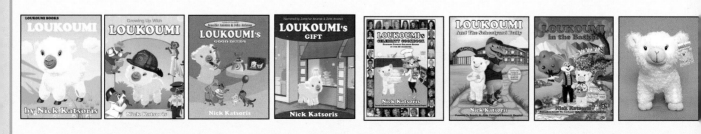

Dedication

Special thanks to Bob Costas for bringing *Loukoumi Saves A Park* to life with his amazing narration, and thank you to everyone for making a difference with Loukoumi.

ABOUT THE NARRATOR

Bob Costas has won 28 Emmy awards – more than any sports broadcaster and he is the only person ever to have won Emmys in news, sports, and entertainment. Bob's peers have named him the "National Sportscaster of the Year" a record eight times, and in 2012, he was elected to the National Sportscasters and Sportswriters Hall of Fame. In the summer of 2018, Bob was also inducted into the broadcaster's ring of the Baseball Hall of Fame.

From the "Baseball Game of the Week" in the 1980s, through his hosting of the Olympics, the late night interview program "Later…with Bob Costas," his programs on HBO, and more, Bob has been a prominent part of the coverage of every major sport over the past three decades. The 2016 Rio, Brazil Summer Olympic Games were Bob's 12th for NBC. Additionally, he has hosted seven Super Bowls, and has been part of the coverage as either play-by play announcer, or host of seven World Series, and ten NBA Finals. Bob has been a prominent part of NBC's presentations of other major events, including the Kentucky Derby, Preakness, and Belmont Stakes, as well as the U. S. Open Golf Championship. Bob has also increased his presence at MLBN, where he has been able to return to his first love, baseball – contributing interviews, commentaries, and play-by-play to the network. He also continues to contribute to NBC News programs, such as "Nightly News" and the "Today Show," and makes special appearances on major events for NBC Sports.

Bob is a native of Queens, New York and grew up on Long Island. He attended Syracuse University in New York, where he majored in communications.

To download Bob Costas' narration, visit www.LoukoumiFoundation.org

LOUKOUMI
Saves A Park

Narrated by
BOB COSTAS

Nick Katsoris